CW00866733

Before reading

Look at the book cove

Ask, "What do you thi

To build independence, tne Level o ...,   d
at the start of this book. If the child needs extra practice, turn
back to pages 6 and 7 in 3a and read the words again with
the child.

During reading

Offer plenty of support and praise as the child reads the story.
Listen carefully and respond to events in the text.

When a **Key Word** is used for the first time, it is also shown at
the bottom of the page. If the child hesitates over a word, point
to the **New Key Words** box and practise reading it together.
If the word is phonically decodable, you can sound out the
letters and blend the sounds to read the word ("d-o-g, dog").
Praise the child for their effort, then return to the story.

Pause every few pages and ask questions to check the child's
understanding of what they have read. If they begin to lose
concentration, stop reading and save the page for later.

Celebrate the child's achievement and come back to the
story the next day.

After reading

After reading this book, ask, "Did you enjoy the story? What did
you like about it?" Encourage the child to share their opinions.

Use the comprehension questions on page 54 to check the
child's understanding and recall of the text.

Ladybird

Series Consultant: Professor David Waugh
With thanks to Kulwinder Maude

LADYBIRD BOOKS

UK | USA | Canada | Ireland | Australia
India | New Zealand | South Africa

Ladybird Books is part of the Penguin Random House group of companies
whose addresses can be found at global.penguinrandomhouse.com.
www.penguin.co.uk   www.puffin.co.uk   www.ladybird.co.uk

 Penguin
Random House
UK

Original edition of Key Words with Peter and Jane first published by Ladybird Books Ltd 1964
Series updated 2023
This book first published 2023
002

Printed in China

The authorized representative in the EEA is Penguin Random House Ireland,
Morrison Chambers, 32 Nassau Street, Dublin D02 YH68

A CIP catalogue record for this book is available from the British Library

ISBN: 978-0-241-51080-3

All correspondence to:
Ladybird Books
Penguin Random House Children's
One Embassy Gardens, 8 Viaduct Gardens, London SW11 7BW

MIX
Paper from
responsible sources
FSC® C018179
FSC
www.fsc.org

Key Words

with Peter and Jane

3b

We can fix it!

Based on the original
Key Words with Peter and Jane
reading scheme and research by William Murray

Original edition written by William Murray
This edition written by Chitra Soundar
Illustrated by Nuno Alexandre Vieira, Flora Aranyi,
and Fran and David Brylewski
Based on characters and design by Gustavo Mazali

Peter plays with cars at home.

Jane looks at a book.

New Key Words

play　　with　　car　　at　　home

Peter and Dad go to play with Tess.

Peter likes playing. He has a ball and a car.

New Key Words

dad   go   to   he

Dad plays with Tess.

"Look at that rabbit, Dad!" Peter says.

Tess goes to get the rabbit.

"No, Tess, please!" Peter says.

"This ball is for you,
Tess. No rabbits!"
Dad says.

"Yes, no rabbits!"
Peter says.

Mum wants to fix the car.

"Can we fix it, Jane?" she says.

"Yes!" says Jane.

"We can look at this car book," says Mum.

"That looks like this car," Jane says.

Jane looks into the car with Mum.

"We can check this," Mum says.

Jane gets water for the car.

Mum tips the water into the car.

Mum gets into the car. "Please go, car!" says Mum.

"We can fix it!" Jane says.

"I want to fix this," Jane says.

She taps the bell, and it falls.

"No!" says Jane.

27

"And I want to look at this," Jane says.

She pulls it.

"No!" says Jane.

29

Mum looks at
the bell.

"We can fix this!"
Mum says.

Dad gets home
with Peter and Tess.

"Have you fixed the
car?" he says.

"No," Jane says.

"We played with Tess," says Peter.

"And a rabbit!" Dad says.

"Look at this bell, Dad," Jane says.

"We can fix it," he says.

Tess gets into
the car.

"No playing in the
car, please, Tess!"
says Dad.

New Key Words

"Jane and Peter, you can go and play," says Mum.

"No, we want to fix this," they say.

"I can look at this with you, Jane," Mum says.

She fixes it.

"Yes, Mum!" says Jane.

43

"I can look at the bell," Dad says.

The bell rings.

"Yes, Dad!" says Peter.

"Quick! Get into the car. Go, go, go!" Mum says.

47

"We can look at the car book," Mum says.

Mum and Dad go and look into the car.

"Can you get that?" Mum says.

Dad tugs at a rag.

Mum and Dad tug.

"That is Tess's rabbit!" Jane says.

"And we fixed the car!" says Peter.

Answer these questions about
the story.

1 What does Peter have with him
   on the walk?

2 What does Mum want to fix?

3 Why does the family get into
   the car?

4 What do Mum and Dad find in the
   car at the end of the story?